The Adventures of Chatterer the Red Squirrel

By THORNTON W. BURGESS

Illustrated by HARRISON CADY

PUBLISHERS

Grosset & Dunlap

NEW YORK

Contents

CONTENTS

[*vi*]

Illustrations

[*vii*]

ILLUSTRATIONS

The Adventures of
Chatterer the Red Squirrel

"Ho!" cried Sammy, "this is important."

I

Chatterer the Red Squirrel Runs for His Life

CHATTERER THE RED SQUIRREL had been scolding because there was no excitement. He had even tried to make some excitement by waking Bobby Coon and making him so angry that Bobby had threatened to eat him alive. It had been great fun to dance around and call Bobby names and make fun of him. Oh, yes, it had been great fun. You see, he knew all the time that Bobby couldn't catch him if he should try. But now things were different. Chatterer had all the excitement that he wanted. Indeed, he had more than he wanted. The truth is, Chatterer was running for his life, and he knew it.

It is a terrible thing, a very terrible thing, to have to run for one's life. Peter Rabbit knows all about it. He has run for his life often. Sometimes it has been Reddy Fox behind him, sometimes Bowser the Hound, and once or twice Old Man Coyote. Peter has known that on his long

[*12*]

legs his life has depended, and more than once a terrible fear has filled his heart. But Peter has also known that if he could reach the old stone wall or the dear Old Briar-patch first, he would be safe, and he always has reached it. So when he has been running with that terrible fear in his heart, there has always been hope there, too.

But Chatterer the Red Squirrel was running without hope. Yes, Sir, there was nothing but fear, terrible fear, in his heart, for he knew not where to go. The hollow tree or the holes in the old stone wall where he would

[13]

be safe from anyone else, even Farmer Brown's boy, offered him no safety now, for the one who was following him with hunger in his anger-red eyes could go anywhere that he could go—could go into any hole big enough for him to squeeze into. You see, it was Shadow the Weasel from whom Chatterer was running, and Shadow is so slim that he can slip in and out of places that even Chatterer cannot get through.

Chatterer knew all this, and so, because it was of no use to run to his usual safe hiding places, he ran in just the other direction. He didn't know where he was going. He had just one thought: to

HARRISON CADY

*It was Shadow the Weasel from whom Chatterer
was running*

run and run as long as he could and then, well, he would try to fight, though he knew it would be of no use.

"Oh dear! Oh dear!" he sobbed, as he ran out on the branch of a tree and leaped across to the next tree, "I wish I had minded my own business! I wish I had kept my tongue still. Shadow the Weasel wouldn't have known where I was if he hadn't heard my voice. Oh dear! Oh dear me! What can I do? What can I do?"

Now in his great fright Chatterer had run and jumped so hard that he was beginning to grow very tired. Presently he found that he must make a very long jump to reach the next tree. He had often made as long a jump as this and thought nothing of it, but now he was so tired that the distance looked twice as great as it really was. He didn't dare stop to run down the tree and scamper across. So he took a long breath, ran swiftly along the branch, and leaped. His hands just touched the tip of the nearest branch of the other tree. He tried his very best to hold on, but he couldn't. Then down, down, down he fell. He spread himself out as flat as he could, and that saved him a little, but still it was a dreadful fall, and when he landed, it seemed for just a minute as if all the breath was gone from his body. But it wasn't quite, and in another minute he was scrambling up the tree.

II

Chatterer's Last Chance

CHATTERER, still running for his life and without the least hope, suddenly saw a last chance to escape from Shadow the Weasel. That is, he saw something that might offer him a chance. He couldn't be sure until he had tried, and even then he might escape from one danger only to run right into another equally great. What Chatterer saw was a big brown bunch near the top of a tall chestnut tree, and he headed for that tree as fast as ever he could go. What was that big brown bunch? Why, it was Redtail the Hawk, who was dozing there with his head drawn down between his shoulders, dreaming.

Now old Redtail is one of Chatterer's deadliest enemies. He is quite as fond of Red Squirrel as is Shadow the Weasel, though he doesn't often try to catch one, because there are other things to eat much easier to get. Chatterer had had more than one narrow escape from old Redtail and was very much afraid of him, yet here he was running up the very tree in which Redtail was sitting. You see, a very daring idea had come into his head. He had seen at once that Redtail was dozing and hadn't seen him at all. He knew that Redtail would just as soon have Shadow the Weasel for dinner as himself, and a very daring plan had popped into his head.

"I may as well be caught by Redtail as Shadow," he thought, as he ran up the tree, "but if my plan works out right, I won't be caught by either. Anyway, it is my very last chance."

Up the tree he scrambled, and after him went Shadow the Weasel. Shadow had been so intent on catching Chatterer that he had not noticed old R. tail, which was just as Chatterer had hoped. Up, up he scrambled, straight past old Redtail, but as he passed, he pulled one of Redtail's long tail feathers, and then ran on to the top of the tree, and with the last bit of strength he had left, leaped to a neighboring spruce tree where, hidden by the thick branches, he stopped to rest and see what would happen.

Of course, when he felt his tail pulled, old Redtail was wide awake in a flash; and of course he looked down to see who had dared to pull his tail. There just below him was

Shadow the Weasel, who had just that minute discovered who was sitting there. Old Redtail hissed sharply, and the feathers on the top of his head stood up in a way they do when he is angry. And he was angry—very angry.

Shadow the Weasel stopped short. Then, like a flash, he dodged around to the other side of the tree. He had no thought of Chatterer now. Things were changed all in an instant, quite changed. Instead of the hunter, he was now the hunted. Old Redtail circled in the air just overhead, and every time he caught sight of Shadow, he swooped at him with great, cruel claws spread to clutch him. Shadow dodged around the trunk of the tree. He was more angry than frightened, for his sharp eyes had spied a little hollow in a branch of the chestnut tree, and he knew that once inside of that, he would have nothing to fear. But he was angry clear through to think that he should be cheated out of that dinner he had been so sure of only a few minutes before. So he screeched angrily at old Redtail and then, watching his chance, scampered out to the hollow and whisked inside, just in the nick of time.

Chatterer, watching from the spruce tree, gave a great sigh of relief. He saw Redtail the Hawk post himself on the top of a tall tree where he could keep watch of that hollow in which Shadow had disappeared, and he knew that it would be a long time before Shadow would dare poke even his nose outside. Then, as soon as he was rested, Chatterer stole softly, oh, so softly, away through the treetops until he was sure that Redtail could not see him. Then he hurried. He wanted to get just as far away from Shadow the Weasel as he could.

III

Chatterer Tells Sammy Jay About Shadow the Weasel

CHATTERER hurried through the Green Forest. He didn't know just where he was going. He had but one thought, and that was to get as far away from Shadow the Weasel as he could. It made him have cold shivers all over every time he thought of Shadow.

"Seems to me you are in a great

hurry," said a voice from a pine tree he was passing.

Chatterer knew that voice without looking to see who was speaking. Everybody in the Green Forest knows that voice. It was the voice of Sammy Jay.

"It looks to me as if you were running away from someone," jeered Sammy.

Chatterer wanted to stop and pick a quarrel with Sammy, as he usually did when they met, but the fear of Shadow the Weasel was still upon him.

"I—I—am," he said in a very low voice.

Sammy looked as if he thought

[27]

he hadn't heard right. Never before had he known Chatterer to admit that he was afraid, for you know Chatterer is a great boaster. It must be something very serious to frighten Chatterer like that.

"What's that?" Sammy asked sharply. "I always knew you to be a coward, but this is the first time I have ever known you to admit it. Whom are you running away from?"

"Shadow the Weasel," replied Chatterer, still in a very low voice, as if he were afraid of being overheard. "Shadow the Weasel is back in the Green Forest, and I have just had such a narrow escape!"

"What's that?" Sammy asked sharply

"Ho!" cried Sammy, "this is important. I thought Shadow was up in the Old Pasture. If he has come back to the Green Forest, folks ought to know it. Where is he now?"

Chatterer stopped and told Sammy all about his narrow escape and how he had left Shadow the Weasel in a hollow of a chestnut tree with Redtail the Hawk watching for him to come out. Sammy's eyes sparkled when Chatterer told how he had pulled the tail of old Redtail. "And he doesn't know now who did it; he thinks it was Shadow," concluded Chatterer, with a weak little grin.

"Ho, ho, ho! Ha, ha, ha!" laughed Sammy Jay. "I wish I had been there to see it."

Then he suddenly grew grave. "Other folks certainly ought to know that Shadow is back in the Green Forest," said he, "so that they may be on their guard. Then if they get caught, it is their own fault. I think I'll go spread the news." You see, for all his mean ways, Sammy Jay does have some good in him, just as everybody does, and he dearly loves to tell important news.

"I—I wish you would go first of all and tell my cousin, Happy Jack the Gray Squirrel," said

[31]

Chatterer, speaking in a hesitating way.

Sammy Jay leaned over and looked at Chatterer sharply. "I thought you and Happy Jack were not friends," said he. "You always seem to be quarreling."

Chatterer looked a little confused, but he is very quick with his tongue, is Chatterer. "That's just it," he replied quickly. "That's just it! If anything should happen to Happy Jack, I wouldn't have him to quarrel with, and it is such fun to see him get mad!"

Now, of course, the real reason why Chatterer wanted Happy Jack warned was because down inside he was ashamed of a dreadful thought that had come to him of leading Shadow the Weasel to Happy Jack's house, so that he himself might escape. It had been a dreadful thought, a cowardly thought, and Chatterer had been really ashamed that he should have ever had such a thought. He thought now that if he could do something for Happy Jack, he would feel better about it.

Sammy Jay promised to go straight to Happy Jack and warn him that Shadow the Weasel was back in the Green Forest, and off he started, screaming the news as he flew, so that all the little people in the Green Forest might know. Chatterer listened a few minutes and then started on.

"Where shall I go?" he muttered. "Where shall I go? I don't dare stay in the Green Forest, for now Shadow will never rest until he catches me."

IV

Chatterer Leaves the Green Forest

CHATTERER was in a peck of trouble. Yes, Sir, he was in a peck of trouble. There was no doubt about it. "Oh dear! Oh dear! If only I had kept my tongue still! If only I had kept my tongue still!" he kept saying over and over to himself, as he hurried through the Green Forest. You see, Chatterer was just beginning to realize what a lot of trouble an unruly tongue can get one into. Here it was cold weather, the very edge of winter, and Chatterer didn't dare stay in the Green Forest where he had always made his home. His store-houses were full of nuts and seeds and corn, enough and more than enough to keep him in comfort all winter, and now he must turn his back on them and go he didn't know where, and all because of his mean disposition and bad tongue.

If he hadn't called Bobby Coon names that morning at the top of his voice, Shadow the Weasel might not have found him. He knew that Shadow has a long memory, and that he would never forget the trick by which Chatterer had escaped, and so the only way Chatterer would ever be able to have a moment's peace would be to leave the Green Forest for as long as Shadow the Weasel chose to stay there. Chatterer shivered inside his warm, red fur coat as he thought of the long, cold winter and how hard it would be to find enough to eat. Was ever anyone else in such a dreadful fix?

Presently he came to the edge of the Green Forest. He sat down

HARRISON CADY

If only he hadn't called Bobby Coon names
at the top of his voice!

to rest in the top of a tree where he could look off over the Green Meadows. Far, far away he could see the Purple Hills, behind which jolly, round, red Mr. Sun goes to bed every night. He could see the old stone wall that separates Farmer Brown's cornfield from the Green Meadows. He could see Farmer Brown's house and barn and near them the Old Orchard where Johnny Chuck had spent the summer with Polly Chuck and their baby Chucks. He knew every nook and corner in the old stone wall and many times he had been to the Old Orchard. It was there that he had stolen the eggs of Drummer the Woodpecker. He grinned at the thought of those eggs and how he had stolen them, and then he shivered as he remembered how he had finally been caught and how sharp the bills of Drummer and Mrs. Drummer were.

But all that was in the past, and thinking about it wasn't going to help him now. He had got to do something right away. Perhaps he might find a place to live in the old stone wall, and there might, there just might, be enough grains of corn scattered over the ground of the cornfield for him to lay up a supply, if he worked very hard and fast. Anyway, he would have a look. So he hurried down from the tree and out along the old stone wall. His spirits began to rise as he whisked along, peering into every hole and jumping from stone to stone. It really seemed as though he might find a snug home somewhere here. Then he remembered something that made his heart sink again. He remembered having seen Shadow the Weasel more than once exploring that very wall. Just as likely as not he would do it again, for it was so very near the Green Forest. No, the old stone wall wouldn't do.

Just then along came Peter

Rabbit. Peter saw right away that something was wrong with Chatterer, and he wanted to know what it was. Chatterer told him. He felt that he had just got to tell someone. Peter looked thoughtful. He scratched his long left ear with his long right hind foot.

"You know there is another old stone wall up there by the Old Orchard," said he. "It is pretty near Farmer Brown's house, and Black Pussy hunts there a great deal, but you ought to be smart enough to keep out of her clutches."

"I should hope so!" exclaimed Chatterer scornfully. "I have never

HARRISON CADY

Just then along came Peter Rabbit

seen a cat yet that I was afraid of! I believe I'll go over and have a look at that old wall, Peter Rabbit."

"I'll go with you," said Peter, and off they started together.

V

Chatterer
Finds a Home

When your plans are upset and all
scattered about,
Just make up your mind that you'll
find a way out.

PETER RABBIT went straight over
to the old stone wall on the
edge of the Old Orchard, lip-
perty-lipperty-lip so fast that it
didn't take him long to get there.
But Chatterer the Red Squirrel
never feels really safe on the

ground unless there is something to climb close at hand, so he went a long way round by way of the rail fence. He always did like to run along a rail fence, and he wouldn't have minded it a bit this morning if he hadn't been in such a hurry. It seemed to him that he never would get there. But, of course, he did.

When he did get there, he found Peter Rabbit sitting on Johnny Chuck's doorstep, staring down Johnny Chuck's long hall. "They're asleep," said he, as Chatterer came up all out of breath. "I've thumped and thumped and thumped, but it isn't the least bit of use. They are asleep, and they'll stay asleep until Mistress Spring arrives. I can't understand it at all. No, Sir, I can't understand how anybody can be willing to miss this splendid cold weather."

Peter shook his head in a puzzled way and continued to stare down the long, empty hall. Of course, he was talking about Johnny and Polly Chuck, who had gone to sleep for the winter. That sleeping business always puzzles Peter. It seems to him like a terrible waste of time. But Chatterer had too much on his mind to waste time wondering how other people could sleep all winter. He couldn't himself, and now that he had been driven away from his own home in the Green Forest by fear of Shadow the Weasel, he couldn't waste a minute. He must find a new home and then spend every minute of daytime laying up a new store of food for the days when everything would be covered with snow.

Up and down the length of the stone wall he scampered, looking for a place to make a home, but nothing suited him. You know he likes best to make his home in a tree. He isn't like Striped Chipmunk, who lives in the ground. Poor Chatterer! He just couldn't see how he was going to live in the old stone wall. He sat on top of a big stone to rest and think it over. He was discouraged. Life didn't seem worth the living just then. He felt as if his heart had gone way down to his toes. Just then his eyes saw something that made his heart come up again with a great bound right where it ought to be, and just then Peter Rabbit came hopping along.

"Have you found a new home yet?" asked Peter.

"Yes," replied Chatterer, "I think I have."

[49]

"That's good," replied Peter. "I was sure you would find one over here. Where is it?"

Chatterer opened his mouth to tell Peter and then closed it with a snap. He remembered just in time how hard it is for Peter to keep a secret. If he should tell Peter, it would be just like Peter to tell someone else without meaning to, and then it might get back to Shadow the Weasel.

"I'm not going to tell you now, Peter Rabbit," said he. "You see, I don't want anybody to know where it is until I am sure that it will do. But I'll tell you this much," he added, as he saw how disappointed Peter looked, "I'm going to live right here."

Peter brightened up right away. You see, he thought that, of course, Chatterer meant that he had found a hole in the old stone wall, and he felt very sure that he could find it by keeping watch. "That's good," he said again. "I'll come see you often. But watch out for Black Pussy; her claws are very sharp. Now I think I'll be going back to the Old Briar-patch."

"Don't tell where I am," called Chatterer.

VI

Peter Rabbit Listens to the Wrong Voice

PETER RABBIT didn't play fair. No, Sir, Peter didn't play fair. People who have too much curiosity about other people's affairs seldom do play fair. He didn't mean to be unfair. Oh, my, no! Peter didn't mean to be unfair. When he left Chatterer the Red Squirrel sitting on the old stone wall on the edge of Farmer Brown's Old Orchard, he intended to go straight home to the dear Old Briar-patch. He was a little disappointed, was Peter, that Chatterer hadn't told him just where his new house was. Not that it really mattered; he just wanted to know, that was all. With every jump away from the old stone wall, that desire to know just where Chatterer's new house was seemed to grow. Peter stopped and looked back. He couldn't see Chatterer now, because the bushes hid him. And if he couldn't see Chatterer, why, of course, Chatterer couldn't see him.

Peter sat down and began to

pull his whiskers in a way he has when he is trying to decide something. It seemed as if two little voices were quarreling inside him. "Go along home like the good fellow you are and mind your own business," said one. "Steal back to the old wall and watch Chatterer and so find out just where his new house is; he'll never know anything about it, and there'll be no harm done," said the other little voice. It was louder than the first voice, and Peter liked the sound of it.

"I believe I will," said he, and without waiting to hear what the

[54]

first little voice would say to that, he turned about and very carefully and softly tiptoed back to the old stone wall. Right near it was a thick little bush. It seemed to Peter that it must have grown there just to give him a hiding place. He crawled under it and lay very flat. He could see along the old stone wall in both directions. Chatterer was sitting just where he had left him. He was looking in the direction that Peter had gone when he had said good-by. Peter chuckled to himself. "He's waiting to make sure I have gone before he goes to

[55]

*Chatterer was sitting just where Peter
had left him*

that new house of his," thought Peter. "This is the time I'll fool him."

"You ought to be ashamed of yourself, Peter Rabbit; this is none of your business," said that little small voice.

"You're not doing a bit of harm. Chatterer has no business to try to keep his new house a secret, anyway," said the other little voice inside. And because of his dreadful curiosity, Peter liked the sound of that voice best and listened to it, and after a while the first voice grew discouraged and stopped.

Chatterer sat where he was for what seemed to Peter a very long time. But by and by he gave a sudden funny little flirt of his tail and ran along the old wall a little way. Then with a hasty look around, he disappeared in a hole. A minute later he popped his head out for another look around and then disappeared again. He did this two or three times as if anxious.

Peter chuckled to himself. "That's his new house right there," said he to himself, "and now that I know where it is, I think I'll hurry along home to the dear Old Briar-patch." He was just getting ready to start when Chatterer popped out of his hole and sat up on a big stone. He was talking out loud, and Peter listened. Then his long ears began to burn, for this is what he heard:

"I'm glad that Peter's not a spy,
    For spies are hateful as can be;
It's dreadful how some people try
    Affairs of other folks to see."

Chatterer whisked out of sight, and Peter hurried to get away. His ears still burned, and somehow he didn't feel so tickled over the thought that he had discovered Chatterer's secret as he had thought he would. And over in the hole in the old stone wall

Chatterer the Red Squirrel was laughing as if there was some great joke. There was, and the joke was on Peter Rabbit. You see, he hadn't discovered Chatterer's new house at all.

VII

How Chatterer Had Fooled Peter Rabbit

CHATTERER THE RED SQUIRREL is a scamp himself and not to be trusted. Nobody in the Green Forest or on the Green Meadows trusts him. And people who cannot be trusted themselves never trust anyone else. Chatterer never does. He is always suspicious. So when Peter Rabbit had said good-by and started for the dear Old Briar-patch without knowing where Chatterer's new house was, Chatterer had made up his mind right away that Peter would never be satisfied until he knew, or thought he knew, where that new house was. You see, he knew all about Peter's dreadful curiosity.

He watched Peter out of sight, then he slipped down out of sight himself between the stones of the old wall. "I know what Peter will do," said he to himself. "Peter will come sneaking back, and hide where he can watch me, and so find out where my new house is. I'll just stay here long enough to give him a chance to hide, and then I'll fool him."

You see, Chatterer knew that if he had been in Peter's place, he would have done just that thing. So he waited a little while and then went back to the place where Peter had left him. There he sat and pretended to be looking in the direction in which Peter had gone, as if to make sure that Peter was really on his way home. But all the time Chatterer was watching out of the corners of his eyes to see if Peter was hiding anywhere near. He didn't see Peter, but he didn't have the least doubt that Peter was somewhere about.

After a while, he ran over to a

hole between the stones of the old wall and pretended to be very busy there, just as if it really were the new house he had found. He kept popping in and out and looking around as if afraid that someone was watching him. He even got some dry leaves and took them inside, as if to make a bed. All the time, although he hadn't seen a sign of Peter, he didn't have the least doubt in the world that Peter was watching him. When he grew tired, a new idea popped into his shrewd little head. He popped out of the hole and sat up on the wall. Then he said aloud that verse which had made Peter's ears burn so. He had meant to make Peter's ears burn. He said that verse just as if he really did believe that Peter was not spying on him and was glad of it. When he had finished, he whisked out of sight again to give Peter a chance to get away. But this time Chatterer did some peeking himself. He hid where Peter couldn't see him, but where he himself could see both ways along the old stone wall, and so it was that he saw Peter crawl out from under the little bush where he had been hiding and sneak away in the direction of the Old Briar-patch. And he knew that this time Peter had gone for good.

Then Chatterer laughed and laughed to think how he had fooled Peter Rabbit, and wished that he could pat himself on the back for being so smart. He didn't once think of how dishonest and mean it was of Peter to spy on him, because, you see, he would have done the same thing himself. "One has to have one's wits very sharp these days to keep a secret," chuckled Chatterer.

But over in the Old Briar-patch that afternoon Peter Rabbit sat very thoughtful and very much ashamed. The thought that he had found out where Chatterer's new house was didn't give him the pleasure that he had thought it would. His ears still burned, for he thought that Chatterer supposed him honest when he wasn't.

"I believe I'll go over tomorrow and tell Chatterer all about it and how mean I have been," said he at last. And when he had made up his mind to do this, he felt better.

And all the time he hadn't found Chatterer's new house at all. You see, it was the old home of Drummer the Woodpecker in an old apple tree which Chatterer had decided to live in.

VIII

Chatterer
Grows Careless

When you grow careless even though
  It be in matters small,
Old Mr. Trouble you will find
  Is bound to make a call.

SOME people never seem to
learn that. You would suppose that after all the trouble
and worry Chatterer the Red
Squirrel had had, he would have
learned a lesson. For a while it
seemed as if he had. Morning
after morning, before anybody

was up in Farmer Brown's house, he visited Farmer Brown's corn-crib, taking the greatest care not to be seen and to get back to his home in the Old Orchard before it was time for Farmer Brown's boy to come out and do his morning's work. And in the corn-crib he took the greatest care to steal only where what he took would not be missed. The empty cobs from which he had eaten the corn he hid in the darkest corner behind the great pile of yellow corn, where they would not be found until nearly all the corn had been taken from the crib. Oh, he was very sly and crafty, was Chatterer the Red Squirrel—at first.

But after a while, when nothing happened, Chatterer grew careless. At first it had seemed very dangerous to go over to the corncrib, but after he had been there often, it didn't seem dangerous at all. Once inside, he would just give himself up to having a good time. He raced about over the great pile of beautiful yellow corn and found the loveliest hiding places in it. Down in a dark corner he made a splendid bed from pieces of husk which hadn't been stripped from some of the ears. It was quite the nicest place he had ever dreamed of, was Farmer Brown's corncrib. He got to feeling that it was his own and not Farmer Brown's at all.

The more that feeling grew, the more careless Chatterer became. He dropped a grain of corn now and then and was too lazy to go down and pick it up, or else didn't think anything about it. Farmer Brown's boy, coming every morning for corn for the hens, noticed these grains, but supposed they were some that had been rubbed from the ears during the handling of them. Then one morning Chatterer dropped a cob from which he had eaten all the corn. He meant to get it and hide it, as he had hidden other cobs, but he didn't want to do it just then. And later —well, then he forgot all about it. Yes, Sir, he forgot all about it until he had reached his home in the Old Orchard.

"Oh, well," thought Chatterer, "it doesn't matter. I can get it and hide it tomorrow morning."

Now a corncob is a very simple thing. Farmer Brown's boy knew where there was a whole pile of them. He added to that pile every day, after shelling enough corn for the biddies. So it would seem that there was nothing about a corncob to make him open his eyes as he did that morning, when he saw the one left by Chatterer the Red Squirrel. But, you see, he knew that a bare corncob had no business inside the corncrib, and suddenly those scattered grains of corn had a new meaning for him.

"Ha, ha!" he exclaimed, "a thief has been here, after all! I thought we were safe from rats and mice, and I don't see now how they got in, for I don't, I really don't, see how they could climb the stone legs of the corncrib. But someone with sharp teeth certainly has been in here. It must be that I have left the door open some time, and a rat has slipped in. I'll just have to get after you, Mr. Rat or Mr. Mouse. We can't have you in our corncrib."

With that he went into the house. Presently he came back, and in one hand was a rattrap and in the other a mousetrap.

IX

Chatterer Grows Too Curious

EVERYBODY knows how curious Peter Rabbit is. He is forever poking his wobbly little nose in where it has no business to be, and as a result Peter is forever getting into trouble. Whenever Chatterer the Red Squirrel has heard a new story about Peter and the scrapes his curiosity has got him into, Chatterer has said that Peter got no more than he deserved. As for himself, he might be curious about a thing he saw for the first time, but he had too much sense to meddle with it until he knew all about it. So Chatterer has come to be thought very smart, quite too smart to be caught in a trap—at least to be caught in an ordinary trap.

Now a great many people manage to make their neighbors think they are a great deal smarter than they really are, and Chatterer is one of this kind. If some of his neighbors could have peeped into Farmer Brown's corncrib the morning after

Farmer Brown's boy found the telltale corncob so carelessly dropped by Chatterer, they would have been surprised. Yes, Sir, they would have been surprised. They would have seen Chatterer the Red Squirrel, the boaster, he of the sharp wits, showing quite as much curiosity as ever possessed Peter Rabbit.

Chatterer had come over to the corncrib as usual to get his daily supply of corn. As usual, he had raced about over the great pile of yellow corn. Quite suddenly his sharp eyes spied something that they hadn't seen before. It was down on the floor of the corn-

HARRISON CADY

Chatterer had come over to the corncrib
as usual

crib quite near the door. Chatterer was sure that it hadn't been there the day before. It was a very queer-looking thing, very queer indeed. And then he spied another queer-looking thing near it, only this was very much smaller. What could they be? He looked at them suspiciously. They looked harmless enough. They didn't move. He ran a few steps towards them and scolded, just as he scolds at anything new he finds out of doors. Still they didn't move. He ran around on a little ledge where he could look right down on the queer things. He was sure now that they were not alive. The biggest one he could see all through. Inside was something to eat. The littlest thing was round and flat with funny bits of wire on top. It looked as if it were made of wood, and in the sides were little round holes too small for him to put his head through.

"Leave them alone," said a small voice inside of Chatterer.

"But I want to see what they are and find out all about them," said Chatterer.

"No good ever comes of meddling with things you don't know about," said the small voice.

"But they are such queer-looking things, and they're not alive.

They can't hurt me," said Chatterer.

Nevertheless he ran back to the pile of corn and tried to eat. Somehow he had lost his appetite. He couldn't take his eyes off those two queer things down on the floor.

"Better keep away," warned the small voice inside.

"It won't do any harm to have a closer look at them," said Chatterer.

So once more he scrambled down from the pile of corn and little by little drew nearer to the two queer things. The nearer he got, the more harmless they looked. Finally he reached out and smelled of the smallest. Then he turned up his nose.

"Smells of mice," muttered Chatterer, "just common barn mice." Then he reached out a paw and touched it. "Pooh!" said he, "it's nothing to be afraid of." Just then he touched one of the little wires, and there was a sudden snap. It frightened Chatterer so that he scurried away. But he couldn't stay away. That snap was such a funny thing, and it hadn't done any harm. You see, he hadn't put his paw in at one of the little holes, or it might have done some harm.

Pretty soon he was back again, meddling with those little wires on top. Every once in a while there would be a snap, and he would scamper away. It was very scary and great fun. By and by the thing wouldn't snap any more, and then Chatterer grew tired of his queer plaything and began to wonder about the other queer thing. No harm had come from the first one, and so he was sure no harm could come from the other.

X

Old Mr. Trouble Gets Chatterer at Last

OF COURSE, you have guessed what it was that Chatterer had been meddling with. It was a mousetrap, and he had sprung it without getting hurt. Chatterer didn't know that it was a trap. He ought to have known, but he didn't. You see, it was not at all like the traps Farmer

Brown's boy had sometimes set for him in the Green Forest. He knew all about those traps and never, never went near them. Now that there was nothing more exciting about the mousetrap, Chatterer turned his attention to the other queer thing. He walked all around it and looked at it from every side. It certainly was queer. Yes, Sir, it certainly was queer! It looked something like a little house only he could see all through it. He put one paw out and touched it. Nothing happened. He tried it again. Then he jumped right on top of it. Still nothing happened. He tried

[*85*]

his sharp teeth on it, but he couldn't bite it. You see, it was made of stout wire.

Inside was something that looked good to eat. It smelled good, too. Chatterer began to wonder what it would taste like. The more he wondered, the more he wanted to know. There must be some way of getting in, and if he could get in, of course, he could get out again. He jumped down to the floor and ran all around the queer little wire house. At each end was a sort of little wire hallway. Chatterer stuck his head in one. It seemed perfectly safe. He crept a little way in and then backed out in a hurry. Nothing happened. He tried it again. Still nothing happened.

"Better keep away," said a small voice down inside of him.

"Pooh! Who's afraid!" said Chatterer. "This thing can't hurt me."

Then he crept a little farther in. Right in front of him was a little round doorway with a little wire door. Chatterer pushed the little door with his nose, and it opened a teeny, weeny bit. He drew back suspiciously. Then he tried it again, and this time pushed the little door a little farther open. He did this two or three times until finally he had his head quite inside, and there, right down below him, was that food he so wanted to taste.

"I can hop right down and get it and then hop right up again," thought Chatterer.

"Don't do it," said the small voice inside. "Corn is plenty good enough. Besides, it is time you were getting back to the Old Orchard."

"It won't take but a minute," said Chatterer, "and I really must know what that tastes like."

With that he jumped down. Snap! Chatterer looked up. The little wire door had closed. Old Mr. Trouble had got Chatterer at last. Yes, Sir, he certainly had got Chatterer this time. You see, he couldn't open that little wire door from the inside. He was in a trap —the wire rattrap set by Farmer Brown's boy.

XI

What Happened Next to Chatterer

WERE you ever terribly, terribly frightened? That was the way Chatterer felt. He was caught; there was no doubt about it! His sharp teeth were of no use at all on those hard wires. He could look out between them, but he couldn't get out. He was too frightened to think. His heart pounded against his sides until it hurt. He forgot all about that queer food he had so wanted to taste, and which was right before him now. Indeed, he felt as if he never, never would want to eat again. What was going to happen to him now? What would Farmer Brown's boy do to him when he found him there?

Hark! What was that? It was a step just outside the door of the corncrib. Farmer Brown's boy was coming! Chatterer raced around his little wire prison and bit savagely at the hard wires. But it was of no use, no use at all. It only hurt his mouth cruelly. Then the door of the corncrib swung open, a flood of light

*Indeed, he felt as if he never would want
to eat again*

poured in, and with it came Farmer Brown's boy.

"Hello!" exclaimed Farmer Brown's boy, as he caught sight of Chatterer. "So you are the thief who has been stealing our corn, and I thought it was a rat or a mouse. Well, well, you little red rascal, didn't you know that thieves come to no good end? You're pretty smart, for I never once thought of you, but you were not so smart as you thought. Now I wonder what we had better do with you."

He picked up the trap with Chatterer in it and stepped out into the beautiful great out-of-doors. Chatterer could see across the dooryard to the Old Orchard and the familiar old stone wall along which he had scampered so often. They looked just the same as ever, and yet—well, they didn't look just the same, for he couldn't look at them without seeing those cruel wires which were keeping him from them.

Farmer Brown's boy put the trap down on the ground and then began to call. "Puss, Puss, Puss," called Farmer Brown's boy. Chatterer's heart, which had been thumping so, almost stopped beating with fright. There was Black Pussy, whom he had so often teased and made fun of. Her yellow eyes had a hungry gleam as she walked around the trap and sniffed and sniffed. Never had Chatterer heard such a terrible sound as those hungry sniffs so close to him! Black Pussy tried to put a paw between the wires, and Chatterer saw the great, cruel claws. But Black Pussy couldn't get her paw between the wires.

"How would you like him for breakfast?" asked Farmer Brown's boy.

"Meow," said Black Pussy, arching her back and rubbing against his legs.

"I suppose that means that you would like him very much,"

laughed Farmer Brown's boy. "Do you think you can catch him if I let him out?"

"Meow," replied Black Pussy again, and to poor Chatterer it seemed the awfullest sound he ever had heard.

"Well, we'll see about it by and by," said Farmer Brown's boy. "There's the breakfast bell, and I haven't fed the biddies yet."

XII

Chatterer Is Sure That This Is His Last Day

THERE was no hope, not the teeniest, weeniest ray of hope in the heart of Chatterer, as Farmer Brown's boy picked up the wire rattrap and started for the house, Black Pussy, the cat, following at his heels and looking up at Chatterer with cruel, hungry eyes. Chatterer took a farewell look at the Old Orchard and way beyond it the Green Forest, from which he had been driven by fear of Shadow the Weasel. Then the door of the farmhouse closed and shut it all out. If there had been any hope in Chatterer's heart, the closing of that door would have shut the last bit out. But there wasn't any hope. Chatterer was sure that he was to be given to Black Pussy for her breakfast.

Farmer Brown's boy put the trap on a table. "What have you there?" called a great voice. It was the voice of Farmer Brown himself, who was eating his breakfast.

"I've got the thief who has been stealing our corn in the crib," replied Farmer Brown's boy, "and who do you think it is?"

"One of those pesky rats," replied Farmer Brown. "I'm afraid you've been careless and left the door open some time, and that is how the rats have got in there."

"But it isn't a rat, and I don't believe that there is a rat there," replied Farmer Brown's boy in triumph. "It's that little scamp of a red squirrel we've seen racing along the wall at the edge of the Old Orchard lately. I can't imagine how he got in there, but there he was, and now here he is."

"What are you going to do with him?" asked Farmer Brown, coming over to look at Chatterer.

"I don't know," replied Farmer Brown's boy, "unless I give him to Black Puss for her breakfast. She has been teasing me for him ever since I found him."

Farmer Brown's boy looked over to the other side of the table as he said this, and his eyes twinkled with mischief.

"Oh, you mustn't do that! That would be cruel!" cried a soft voice. "You must take him down to the Green Forest and let him go." A gentle face with pitying eyes was bent above the trap. "Just see how frightened the poor little thing is! You must take him straight down to the Green Forest right after breakfast."

"Isn't that just like Mother?" cried Farmer Brown's boy. "I believe it would be just the same with the ugliest old rat that ever lived. She would try to think of some excuse for letting it go."

"God made all the little people who wear fur, and they must have some place in His great plan," said Mrs. Brown.

Farmer Brown laughed a big, hearty laugh. "True enough,

Mother!" said he. "The trouble is, they get out of place. Now this little rascal's place is down in the Green Forest and not up in our corncrib."

"Then put him back in his right place!" was the prompt reply, and they all laughed.

Now all this time poor Chatterer was thinking that this surely was his last day. You see, he knew that he had been a thief, and he knew that Farmer Brown's boy knew it. He just crouched down in a little ball, too miserable to do anything but tremble every time anyone came near. He was sure that he had seen for the last time the Green Forest and the

Green Meadows and jolly Mr. Sun and all the other beautiful things he loved so, and it seemed as if his heart would burst with despair.

XIII

Chatterer
Is Put in Prison

Whoever does a deed that's wrong
Will surely find someday
That for that naughty act of his
He'll surely have to pay.

THAT was the way with Chatterer. Of course, he had had no business to steal corn from Farmer Brown's corncrib. To be sure, he had felt that he had just as much right to that corn as Farmer Brown had. You see, the little people of the Green Mead-

ows and the Green Forest feel
that everything that grows be-
longs to them, if they want it
and are smart enough to get it
before someone else does. But
it is just there that Chatterer
went wrong. Farmer Brown had
harvested that corn and stored it
in his corncrib, and so, of course,
no one else had any right to it.
Right down deep in his heart
Chatterer knew this. If he hadn't
known it, he wouldn't have been
so sly in taking what he wanted.
He knew all the time that he was
stealing, but he tried to make
himself believe that it was all
right. So he had kept on stealing

and stealing until at last he was caught in a trap, and now he had got to pay for his wrongdoing.

Chatterer was very miserable, so miserable and frightened that he could do nothing but sit huddled up in a little shivery ball. He hadn't the least doubt in the world that this was his very last day, and that Farmer Brown's boy would turn him over to cruel Black Pussy for her breakfast. Farmer Brown's boy had left him in the trap in the house and had gone out. For a long time Chatterer could hear pounding out in the woodshed, and Farmer

Brown's boy was whistling as he pounded. Chatterer wondered how he could whistle and seem so happy when he meant to do such a dreadful thing as to give him to Black Pussy. After what seemed a very long time, ages and ages, Farmer Brown's boy came back. He had with him a queer-looking box.

"There," said he, "is a new home for you, you little red imp! I guess it will keep you out of trouble for a while."

He slid back a little door in the top of the box, and then, putting on a stout glove and opening a little door in the trap, he put in his big hand and closed it around Chatterer.

Poor little Chatterer! He was sure now that this was the end, and that he was to be given to Black Pussy, who was looking on with hungry, yellow eyes. He struggled and did his best to bite, but the thick glove gave his sharp little teeth no chance to hurt the hand that held him. Even in his terror, he noticed that that big hand tried to be gentle and squeezed him no tighter than was necessary. Then he was lifted out of the trap and dropped through the little doorway in the top of the queer box, and the door was fastened. Nothing terrible had happened, after all.

At first Chatterer just sulked in one corner. He still felt sure that something terrible was going to happen. Farmer Brown's boy took the box out into the shed and put it where the sun shone into it. For a little while he stayed watching, but Chatterer still sulked and sulked. By and by he went away, taking Black Pussy with him, and Chatterer was alone.

When he was quite sure that no one was about, Chatterer began to wonder what sort of a place he was in, and if there wasn't some way to get out. He found that one side and the top were of fine, stout wire, through which he could look out, and that the other sides and the bottom were of wood covered with wire, so that there was no chance for his sharp teeth to gnaw a way out. In one corner was a stout piece of an apple tree, with two little stubby branches to sit on, and halfway up a little round hole. Very cautiously Chatterer peeped inside the hole. Inside was a splendid hollow. On the floor of the box was a little heap of shavings and bits of rag. And there was a little pile of yel-

*Very cautiously Chatterer peeped inside
the hole*

low corn. How Chatterer did hate the sight of that corn! You see, it was corn that had got him into all this trouble. At least, that is the way Chatterer felt about it. When he had examined everything, he knew that there was no way out. Chatterer was in a prison, though that is not what Farmer Brown's boy called it. He said it was a cage.

XIV

Chatterer
Decides To Live

AT FIRST Chatterer decided that he had rather die than live in a prison, no matter how nice that prison might be. It was a very foolish thing to do, but he made up his mind that he just wouldn't eat. He wouldn't touch that nice, yellow corn Farmer Brown's boy had put in his prison for him. He would starve himself to death. Yes, Sir, he would starve himself to death. So when he found that there was no way to get out of his prison, he curled up in the little hollow stump in his prison, where no one could see him, and made up his mind that he would stay there until he died. Life wasn't worth living if he had got to spend all the rest of his days in a prison. He wouldn't even make himself comfortable. There was that little heap of nice shavings and bits of rag for him to make a nice comfortable bed of, but he didn't touch them. No, Sir, he just tried to make himself miserable.

Not once that long day did he poke so much as the tip of his nose out of his little round doorway. Ever so many times Farmer Brown's boy came to see him, and whistled and called softly to him. But Chatterer didn't make a sound. At last night came, and the woodshed where his prison was grew dark and darker and very still. Now it was about this time that Chatterer's stomach began to make itself felt. Chatterer tried not to notice it, but his stomach would be noticed, and Chatterer couldn't help himself. His stomach was empty, and it kept telling him so.

"I'm going to starve to death," said Chatterer to himself over and over.

"I'm empty, and there is plenty of food to fill me up, if you'll only stop being silly," whispered his stomach.

The more Chatterer tried not to think of how good something to eat would taste, the more he did think of it. It made him restless and uneasy. He twisted and squirmed and turned. At last he decided that he would have one more look to see if he couldn't find some way to get out of his prison. He poked his head out of the little round doorway. All was still and dark. He listened, but not a sound could he hear. Then he softly crept out and hurriedly examined all the inside of his prison once more. It was of no use! There wasn't a single place where he could use his sharp teeth.

"There's that little pile of corn waiting for me," whispered his stomach.

"I'll never touch it!" said Chatterer fiercely.

Just then he hit something with his foot, and it rolled. He picked it up and then put it down again. It was a nut, a plump hickory nut. Two or three times he picked it up and put it down, and each time it was harder than before to put it down.

"I—I—I'd like to taste one more nut before I starve to death," muttered Chatterer, and almost without knowing it, he began to gnaw the hard shell. When that nut was finished, he found another; and when that was gone, still another. Then he just had to taste a grain of corn. The first thing Chatterer knew, the nuts and the corn were all gone, and his stomach was full. Somehow he felt ever so much better. He didn't feel like starving to death now.

[118]

"I—I believe I'll wait a bit and see what happens," said he to himself, "and while I'm waiting, I may as well be comfortable."

With that he began to carry the shavings and rags into the hollow stump and soon had as comfortable a bed as ever he had slept on. Chatterer had decided to live.

XV

Farmer Brown's Boy Tries To Make Friends

Nobody lives who's wholly bad;
  Some good you'll find in every heart.
Your enemies will be your friends
  If only you will do your part.

ALL his life Chatterer the Red Squirrel had looked on Farmer Brown's boy as his enemy, just as did all the other little people of the Green Meadows, the Green Forest, and the

Smiling Pool. They feared him, and because they feared him, they hated him. So whenever he came near, they ran away. Now at first Farmer Brown's boy used to run after them for just one thing—because he wanted to make friends with them, and he couldn't see how ever he was going to do it unless he caught them. After a while, when he found that he couldn't catch them by running after them, he made up his mind that they didn't want to be his friends, and so then he began to hunt them, because he thought it was fun to try to outwit them. Of course, when he began to do that, they hated him and feared him all the more. You see, they didn't understand that really he had one of the kindest hearts in the world; and he didn't understand that they hated him just because they didn't know him.

So when Chatterer had been caught in the trap in Farmer Brown's corncrib, he hadn't doubted in the least that Farmer Brown's boy would give him to Black Pussy or do something equally cruel; and even when he found that he was only to be kept a prisoner in a very comfortable prison, with plenty to eat and drink, he wasn't willing to be-

lieve any good of Farmer Brown's
boy. Indeed, he hated him more
than ever, if that were possible.

But Farmer Brown's boy was
very patient. He came to Chatterer's prison ever so many times
a day and whistled and clucked
and talked to Chatterer. And he
brought good things to eat. It
seemed as if he were all the time
trying to think of some new treat
for Chatterer. He never came
without bringing something. At
first Chatterer would hide in his
hollow stump as soon as he saw
Farmer Brown's boy coming and
wouldn't so much as peek out
until he had gone away. When he

was sure that the way was clear, he would come out again, and always he found some delicious fat nuts or some other dainty waiting for him. After a little, as soon as he saw Farmer Brown's boy coming, Chatterer would begin to wonder what good thing he had brought this time, and would grow terribly impatient for Farmer Brown's boy to go away so that he could find out.

By and by it got so that he couldn't wait, but would slyly peep out of his little round doorway to see what had been brought for him. Then one day Farmer Brown's boy didn't come at all.

Chatterer tried to make himself believe that he was glad. He told himself that he hated Farmer Brown's boy, and he hoped that he never, never would see him again. But all the time he knew that it wasn't true. It was the longest day since Chatterer had been a prisoner. Early the next morning, before Chatterer was out of bed, he heard a step in the woodshed, and before he thought what he was doing, he was out of his hollow stump to see if it really was Farmer Brown's boy. It was, and he had three great fat nuts which he dropped into Chatterer's cage. It seemed to Chatterer that he just couldn't wait for Farmer Brown's boy to go away. Finally he darted forward and seized one. Then he scampered to the shelter of his hollow stump to eat it. When it was finished, he just had to have another. Farmer Brown's boy was still watching, but somehow Chatterer didn't feel so much afraid. This time he sat up on one of the little branches of the stump and ate it in plain sight. Farmer Brown's boy smiled, and it was a pleasant smile.

"I believe we shall be friends, after all," said he.

XVI

Chatterer Has a Pleasant Surprise

CHATTERER THE RED SQUIRREL, the mischief maker of the Green Forest, had never been more comfortable in his life. No matter how rough Brother North Wind roared across the Green Meadows and through the Green Forest, piling the snow in great drifts, he couldn't send so much as one tiny shiver through the little red coat of Chatterer. And always right at hand was plenty to eat—corn and nuts and other good things such as Chatterer loves. No, he never had been so comfortable in all his life. But he wasn't happy, not truly happy. You see, he was in prison, and no matter how nice a prison may be, no one can be truly happy there.

Since he had been a prisoner, Chatterer had learned to think very differently of Farmer Brown's boy from what he used to think. In fact, he and Farmer Brown's boy had become very good friends, for Farmer Brown's boy was always very gentle, and always brought him something good to eat.

"He isn't at all like what I had thought," said Chatterer, "and if I were free, I wouldn't be afraid of him at all. I—I'd like to tell some of the other little Green Forest people about him. If only—"

Chatterer didn't finish. Instead a great lump filled his throat. You see, he was thinking of the Green Forest and the Old Orchard, and how he used to race through the treetops and along the stone wall. Half the fun in life had been in running and jumping, and now there wasn't room in this little prison to stretch his legs. If only he could run—run as hard as ever he knew how—once in a while, he felt that his prison wouldn't be quite so hard to put up with.

That very afternoon, while Chatterer was taking a nap in his bed in the hollow stump, something was slipped over his little round doorway, and Chatterer awoke in a terrible fright to find himself a prisoner inside his hollow stump. There was nothing he could do about it but just lie there in his bed, and shake with fright, and wonder what dreadful thing was going to happen next. He could hear Farmer Brown's boy very busy about something in his cage. After a long, long time, his little round doorway let in

the light once more. The door
had been opened. At first Chatterer didn't dare go out, but he
heard the soft little whistle with
which Farmer Brown's boy always
called him when he had something especially nice for him to
eat, so at last he peeped out.
There on the floor of the cage
were some of the nicest nuts.
Chatterer came out at once. Then
his sharp eyes discovered something else. It was a queer-looking
thing made of wire at one end of
his cage.

Chatterer looked at it with
great suspicion. Could it be a new
kind of trap? But what would a
trap be doing there, when he was

already a prisoner? He ate all the nuts, all the time watching this new, queer-looking thing. It seemed harmless enough. He went a little nearer. Finally he hopped into it. It moved. Of course, that frightened him, and he started to run up. But he didn't go up. No, Sir, he didn't go up. You see, he was in a wire wheel; and as he ran, the wheel went around. Chatterer was terribly frightened, and the faster he tried to run, the faster the wheel went around. Finally he had to stop, because he was out of breath and too tired to run another step. When he stopped, the wheel stopped.

Little by little, Chatterer began to understand. Farmer Brown's boy had made that wheel to give him a chance to run all he wanted to and whenever he wanted to. When he understood this, Chatterer was as nearly happy as he could be in a prison. It was such a pleasant surprise! He would race and race in it until he just had to stop for breath. Farmer Brown's boy looked on and laughed to see how much happier he had made Chatterer.

XVII

Sammy Jay's Sharp Eyes

EVERYBODY knows that Sammy Jay has sharp eyes. In fact, there are very few of the little forest people whose eyes are as sharp as Sammy's. That is because he uses them so much. A long time ago he found out that the more he used his eyes, the sharper they became, and so there are very few minutes when Sammy is awake that he isn't trying to see something. He is always looking. That is the reason he always knows so much about what is going on in the Green Forest and on the Green Meadows.

Now, of course, Chatterer the Red Squirrel couldn't disappear without being missed, particularly by Sammy Jay. And, of course, Sammy couldn't miss Chatterer and not wonder what had become of him. At first Sammy thought that Chatterer was hiding, but after peeking and peering and watching in the Old Orchard for a few days, he was forced to think that either Chatterer had

[135]

once more moved or else that something had happened to him.

"Perhaps Shadow the Weasel has caught him, after all," thought Sammy, and straightway flew to a certain place in the Green Forest where he might find Shadow the Weasel. Sure enough, Shadow was there. Now, of course, it wouldn't do to ask right out if Shadow had caught Chatterer, and Sammy was smart enough to know it.

"Chatterer the Red Squirrel sends his respects and hopes you are enjoying your hunt for him," called Sammy.

Shadow looked up at Sammy,

and anger blazed in his little red eyes. "You tell Chatterer that I'll get him yet!" snarled Shadow.

Sammy's eyes sparkled with mischief. He had made Shadow angry, and he had found out what he wanted to know. He was sure that Shadow had not caught Chatterer.

"But what can have become of him?" thought Sammy. "I've got no love for him, but just the same I miss him. I really must find out. Yes, Sir, I really must."

So every minute that he could spare, Sammy Jay spent trying to find Chatterer. He asked every-one he met if they had seen

"You tell Chatterer that I'll get him yet!"
snarled Shadow

Chatterer. He peeked and peered into every hollow and hiding place he could think of. But look as he would and ask as he would, he could find no trace of Chatterer. At last he happened to think of Farmer Brown's corn-crib. Could it be that Chatterer had moved over there or had come to some dreadful end there? Very early the next morning, Sammy flew over to the corn-crib. He looked it all over with his sharp eyes and listened for sounds of Chatterer inside. But not a sound could he hear. Then he remembered the hole under the edge of the roof through which Chatterer used to go in and out. Sammy hurried to look at it. It was closed by a stout board nailed across it. Then Sammy knew that Farmer Brown's boy had found it.

"He's killed Chatterer, that's what he's done!" cried Sammy, and flew over to the Old Orchard filled with sad thoughts. He meant to wait until Farmer Brown's boy came out and then tell him what he thought of him. After that, he would fly through the Green Forest and over the Green Meadows to spread the sad news.

After a while, the door of the farmhouse opened, and Farmer

[*140*]

Brown's boy stepped out. Sammy had his mouth open to scream, when his sharp eyes saw something queer. Farmer Brown's boy had a queer-looking box in his arms which he put on a shelf where the sun would shine on it. It looked to Sammy as if something moved inside that box. He forgot to scream and say the bad things he had planned to say. He waited until Farmer Brown's boy had gone to the barn. Then Sammy flew where he could look right into the queer box. There was Chatterer the Red Squirrel!

XVIII

Chatterer
Is Made Fun of

"HA, HA, HA! Ho, ho, ho! Smarty caught at last!" Sammy Jay fairly shrieked with glee, as he peered down from the top of an apple tree at Chatterer, in the cage Farmer Brown's boy had made for him. Sammy was so relieved to think that Chatterer was not dead, and he was so tickled to think that Chatterer, who always thought himself so smart, should have been caught, that he just had to torment Chatterer by laughing at him and saying mean things to him, until Chatterer lost his temper and said things back quite in the old way. This tickled Sammy more than ever, for it sounded so exactly like Chatterer when he had been a free little imp of mischief in the Green Forest, that Sammy felt sure that Chatterer had nothing the matter with him.

But he couldn't stop very long to make fun of poor Chatterer. In the first place, Farmer Brown's boy had put his head out the barn door to see what all the fuss was about. In the second place, Sammy fairly ached all over to spread the news 'through the Green Forest and over the Green Meadows. You know he is a great gossip. And this was such unusual news. Sammy knew very well that no one would believe him. He knew that they just couldn't believe that smart Mr. Chatterer had really been caught. And no one did believe it.

"All right," Sammy would reply. "It doesn't make the least bit of difference in the world to me whether you believe it or not. You can go up to Farmer Brown's house and see him in prison yourself, just as I did."

So, late that afternoon, when all was quiet around the farmyard, Chatterer saw something very familiar behind the old stone wall at the edge of the Old Orchard. It bobbed up and then dropped out of sight again. Then it bobbed up again, only to drop out of sight just as quickly.

"It looks to me very much as if Peter Rabbit is over there and feeling very nervous," said Chatterer to himself, and then he called sharply, just as when he was free in the Green Forest. Right away Peter's head bobbed up for all the world like a jack-in-the-box, and this time it stayed up. Peter's eyes were round with surprise, as he stared across at Chatterer's prison.

"Oh, it's true!" gasped Peter, as if it were as hard work to believe his own eyes as it was to believe Sammy Jay. "I must go right away and see what can be done to get Chatterer out of trouble." And then, because it was broad daylight, and he really didn't dare stay another minute, Peter waved good-by to Chatterer and started for the Green Forest as fast as his long legs could take him.

A little later who should appear peeping over the stone wall but Reddy Fox. It seemed very bold of Reddy, but really it

HARRISON CADY

*Who should appear peeping over the stone
wall but Reddy Fox*

wasn't nearly as bold as it seemed. You see, Reddy knew that Farmer Brown's boy and Bowser the Hound were over in the Old Pasture, and that he had nothing to fear. He grinned at Chatterer in the most provoking way. It made Chatterer angry just to see him.

"*Smarty, Smarty, Mr. Smarty,*
Glad to see you looking hearty!
Weather's fine, as you can see;
Won't you take a walk with me?"

So said Reddy Fox, knowing all the time that Chatterer couldn't take a walk with anyone. At first Chatterer scolded and called Reddy all the bad names he could think of, but after a little he didn't feel so much like scolding. In fact, he didn't half hear the mean things Reddy Fox said to him. You see, it was coming over him more and more that nothing could take the place of freedom. He had a comfortable home, plenty to eat, and was safe from every harm, but he was a prisoner, and having these visitors made him realize it more than ever. Something very like tears filled his eyes, and he crept into his hollow stump where he couldn't see or be seen.

XIX

Peter Rabbit Tries To Help

PETER RABBIT is one of the kindest-hearted little people of the Green Forest or the Green Meadows. He is happy-go-lucky, and his dreadful curiosity is forever getting him into all kinds of trouble. Perhaps it is because he has been in so many scrapes himself that he always feels sorry for others who get into trouble. Anyway, no sooner does Peter hear of someone in trouble, than he begins to wonder how he can help them. So just as soon as he found out for himself that Sammy Jay had told the truth about Chatterer the Red Squirrel, and that Chatterer really was in a prison at Farmer Brown's house, he began to think and think to find some way to help Chatterer.

Now, of course, Peter didn't know what kind of a prison Chatterer was in. He remembered right away how Prickly Porky the Porcupine had gnawed a great hole in the box in which Johnny Chuck's lost baby was kept by Farmer Brown's boy. Why shouldn't Prickly Porky do as much for Chatterer? He would go see him at once. The trouble with Peter is that he doesn't think of all sides of a question. He is impulsive. That is, he goes right ahead and does the thing that comes into his head first, and sometimes this isn't the wisest or best thing to do. So now he scampered down into the Green Forest as fast as his long legs would carry him, to hunt for Prickly Porky. It was no trouble at all to find him, for he had only to follow the line of trees that had been stripped of their bark.

"Good afternoon, Prickly Porky. Have you heard the news about Chatterer?" said Peter, talking very fast, for he was quite out of breath.

"Yes," replied Prickly Porky. "Serves him right. I hope it will teach him a lesson."

Peter's heart sank. "Don't you think it is dreadful?" he asked. "Just think, he will never, never be able to run and play in the Green Forest again, unless we can get him out."

"So much the better," grunted Prickly Porky. "So much the better. He always was a nuisance. Never did see such a fellow for making trouble for other people.

[*153*]

No, Sir, I never did. The rest of us can have some peace now. Serves him right." Prickly Porky went on chewing bark as if Chatterer's trouble was no concern of his.

Peter's heart sank lower still. He scratched one long ear slowly with a long hind foot, which is a way he has when he is thinking very hard. He was so busy thinking that he didn't see the twinkle in the dull little eyes of Prickly Porky, who really was not so hard-hearted as his words sounded. After a long time, during which Peter thought and thought, and Prickly Porky ate and ate, the latter spoke again.

"What have you got on your mind, Peter?" he asked.

"I—I was just thinking how perfectly splendid it would be if you would go up there and gnaw a way out of his prison for Chatterer," replied Peter timidly.

"Huh!" grunted Prickly Porky. "Huh! Some folks think my wits are pretty slow, but even I know better than that. Put on your thinking cap again, Peter Rabbit."

"Why can't you? You are not afraid of Bowser the Hound or Farmer Brown's boy, and everybody else is, excepting Jimmy Skunk," persisted Peter.

"For the very good reason that

[155]

if I could gnaw into his prison, Chatterer could gnaw out. If he can't gnaw his way out with those sharp teeth of his, I certainly can't gnaw in. Where's your common sense, Peter Rabbit?"

"That's so. I hadn't thought of that," replied Peter slowly and sorrowfully. "I must try to think of some other way to help Chatterer."

"I'd be willing to try if it was of any use. But it isn't," said Prickly Porky, who didn't want Peter to think that he really was as hardhearted as he had seemed at first.

So Peter bade Prickly Porky good-by and started for the dear

HARRISON CADY

"I'd be willing to try if it was of any use,"
said Prickly Porky

Old Briar-patch to try to think of some other way to help Chatterer. On the way he waked up Unc' Billy Possum and Bobby Coon, but they couldn't give him any help. "There really doesn't seem to be any way I can help," sighed Peter. And there really wasn't.

XX

Chatterer Has Another Great Surprise

CHATTERER had never had so many surprises—good surprises—in all his life, as since the day he had been caught in a trap in Farmer Brown's corncrib. In the first place, it had been a great surprise to him that he had not been given to Black Pussy, as he had fully expected to be. Then had come the even greater surprise of finding that Farmer Brown's boy was ever and ever so much nicer than he had thought. A later surprise had been the wire wheel in his cage, so that he could run to his heart's content. It was such a pleasant and wholly unexpected surprise that it had quite changed Chatterer's feelings toward Farmer Brown's boy.

The fact is, Chatterer could have been truly happy but for one thing—he was a prisoner. Yes, Sir, he was a prisoner, and he couldn't forget it for one minute while he was awake. He used to watch Farmer Brown's boy and wish with all his might that he could make him understand how dreadful it was to be in a prison. But Farmer Brown's boy couldn't understand what Chatterer said, no matter how hard Chatterer tried to make him. He seemed to think that Chatterer was happy. He just didn't understand that not all the good things in the world could make up for loss of freedom—that it is better to be free, though hungry and cold. than in a prison with every com-fort.

Chatterer had stood it pretty well and made the best of things until Sammy Jay had found him, and Reddy Fox had made fun of him, and Peter Rabbit had

[*161*]

peeped at him from behind the old stone wall. The very sight of them going where they pleased and when they pleased had been too much for Chatterer, and such a great longing for the Green Forest and the Old Orchard filled his heart that he could think of nothing else. He just sat in a corner of his cage and looked as miserable as he felt. He lost his appetite. In vain Farmer Brown's boy brought him the fattest nuts and other dainties. He couldn't eat for the great longing for freedom that filled his heart until it seemed ready to burst. He no longer cared to run in the new wire wheel which had given him so much pleasure at first. He was homesick, terribly homesick, and he just couldn't help it.

Farmer Brown's boy noticed it, and his face grew sober and thoughtful. He watched Chatterer when the latter didn't know that he was about, and if he couldn't understand Chatterer's talk, he could understand Chatterer's actions. He knew that he was unhappy and guessed why. One morning Chatterer did not come out of his hollow stump as he usually did when his cage was placed on the shelf outside the farmhouse door. He just didn't feel like it. He stayed curled up in his bed for a long, long time, too sad and miserable to move. At last he crawled up and peeped out of his little round doorway. Chatterer gave a little gasp and rubbed his eyes. Was he dreaming? He scrambled out in a hurry and peeped through the wires of his cage. Then he rubbed his eyes again and rushed over to the other side of the cage for another look. His cage wasn't on the usual shelf at all! It was on the snow-covered stone wall at the edge of the Old Orchard.

Chatterer was so excited he didn't know what to do. He raced around the cage. Then he jumped into the wire wheel and made it spin round and round as never before. When he was too tired to run any more, he jumped out. And right then he discovered something he hadn't noticed before. The little door in the top of his cage was open! It must be that Farmer Brown's boy had forgotten to close it when he put in Chatterer's breakfast. Chatterer forgot that he was tired. Like a little red flash he was outside and whisking along the snow-covered stone wall straight for his home in the Old Orchard.

"Chickaree! Chickaree! Chickaree!" he shouted as he ran.

XXI

Chatterer Hears the Small Voice

THE very first of the little meadow and forest people to see Chatterer after he had safely reached the Old Orchard, was Tommy Tit the Chickadee. It just happened that Tommy was very busy in the very apple tree in which was the old home of Drummer the Woodpecker when Chatterer reached it. You know Chatterer had moved into it for the winter just a little while before he had been caught in the corncrib by Farmer Brown's boy.

Yes, Sir, Tommy was very busy, indeed. He was so busy that, sharp as his bright little eyes are, he had not seen Chatterer racing along the snow-covered old stone wall. It wasn't until he heard Chatterer's claws on the trunk of the apple tree that Tommy saw him at all. Then he was so surprised that he lost his balance and almost turned a somersault in the air before he caught another twig. You see, he knew all about Chatterer and how he had

[167]

been kept a prisoner by Farmer Brown's boy.

"Why! Why-ee! Is this really you, Chatterer?" he exclaimed. "How ever did you get out of your prison? I'm glad, ever and ever so glad, that you got away."

Chatterer flirted his tail in the saucy way he has, and his eyes twinkled. Here was just the best chance ever to boast and brag. He could tell Tommy Tit how smart he had been—smart enough to get away from Farmer Brown's boy. Tommy Tit would tell the other little people, and then everybody would think him just as smart as Unc' Billy Possum; and

[*168*]

you know Unc' Billy really was smart enough to get away from Farmer Brown's boy after being caught. Everybody knew that he had been a prisoner, and now that he was free, everybody would believe whatever he told them about how he got away. Was there ever such a chance to make his friends and neighbors say: "What a smart fellow he is!"

"I — I —" Chatterer stopped. Then he began again. "You see, it was this way: I—I—" Somehow, Chatterer couldn't say what he had meant to say. It seemed as if Tommy Tit's bright, merry eyes were looking right into his head and heart and could see his very thoughts. Of course, they couldn't. The truth is that little small voice inside, which Chatterer had so often refused to listen to when he was tempted to do wrong, was talking again. It was saying: "For shame, Chatterer! For shame! Tell the truth. Tell the truth." It was that little small voice that made Chatterer hesitate and stop.

"You don't mean to say that you were smart enough to fool Farmer Brown's boy and get out of that stout little prison he made for you, do you?" asked Tommy Tit.

"No," replied Chatterer, almost before he thought. "No, I didn't. The fact is, Tommy Tit, he left the door open purposely. He let me go. Farmer Brown's boy isn't half so bad as some people think."

"Dee, dee, dee," laughed Tommy Tit. "I've been telling a lot of you fellows that for a long time, but none of you would believe me. Now I guess you know it. Why, I'm not the least bit afraid of Farmer Brown's boy— not the least little bit in the world. If all the little forest and meadow people would only trust him, instead of running away from him, he would be the very best friend we have."

"Perhaps so," replied Chatterer doubtfully. "He was very good to me while I was in his prison, and—and I'm not so very much afraid of him now. Just the same, I don't mean to let him get hands on me again."

"Pooh!" said Tommy Tit. "Pooh! I'd just as soon eat out of his hand."

"That's all very well for you to say, when you are flying around free, but I don't believe you dare go up to his house and prove it," retorted Chatterer.

"Can't now," replied Tommy.

"I've got too much to do for him right now, but someday I'll show you. Dee, dee, dee, chicka-dee! I'm wasting my time talking when there is such a lot to be done. I am clearing his apple trees of insect eggs."

"Ha, ha, ha! Go it, you little red scamp!" shouted a voice behind him.

Then Chatterer knew that Farmer Brown's boy had not left the little door open by mistake, but had given him his freedom, and right then he knew that they were going to be the best of friends.

XXII

Tommy Tit Makes Good His Boast

DEE, dee, dee, chickadee! See me! See me!" Tommy Tit the Chickadee kept saying this over and over, as he flew from the Green Forest up through the Old Orchard on his way to Farmer Brown's dooryard, and his voice was merry. In fact, his voice was the merriest, cheeriest sound to be heard that bright, snapping, cold morning.

To be sure, there were other voices, but they were not merry, nor were they cheery. There was the voice of Sammy Jay, but it sounded peevish and discontented. And there was the voice of Blacky the Crow, but it sounded harsh and unpleasant. And there was the voice of Chatterer the Red Squirrel, but Chatterer was scolding just from habit, and his voice was not pleasant to hear.

So everyone who heard Tommy Tit's cheery voice that cold winter morning just had to smile. Yes, Sir, they just had to smile, even Sammy Jay and

HARRISON CADY

So everyone who heard Tommy Tit's cheery
voice just had to smile

Blacky the Crow. They just couldn't help themselves. When Tommy reached the stone wall that separated the Old Orchard from Farmer Brown's dooryard, his sharp eyes were not long in finding Peter Rabbit and Happy Jack the Gray Squirrel and Chatterer hiding in the old wall where they could peep out and see all that happened in Farmer Brown's dooryard. Looking back through the Old Orchard, he saw what looked like a little bit of the blue, blue sky flitting silently from tree to tree. It was Sammy Jay. Over in the very top of a tall maple tree, a long way off, was a spot of black. Tommy

[*177*]

didn't need to be told that it was Blacky the Crow, who didn't dare come any nearer.

Tommy fairly bubbled over with joy. He knew what it all meant. He knew that Peter Rabbit and Happy Jack and Chatterer and Sammy Jay and Blacky the Crow had come to see him make good his boast to Chatterer that he would eat from the hand of Farmer Brown's boy, and that not one of them really believed that he would do it. He tickled all over and cut up all sorts of capers, just for pure joy. Finally he flew over to the maple tree that grows close by Farmer Brown's house.

"Dee, dee, dee, chickadee! See me! See me!" called Tommy Tit, and his voice sounded cheerier than ever and merrier than ever. Then the door of Farmer Brown's house opened, and out stepped Farmer Brown's boy and looked up at Tommy Tit, and the look in his eyes was gentle and good to see. He pursed up his lips, and from them came the softest, sweetest whistle, and it sounded like "Phoe-be."

Peter Rabbit pinched himself to be sure that he was awake, for it was Tommy Tit's own love note, and if Peter had not been looking straight at Farmer Brown's boy, he would have been

[179]

sure that it was Tommy himself who had whistled.

"Phoe-be," whistled Farmer Brown's boy again.

"Phoe-be," replied Tommy Tit, and it was hard to say which whistle was the softest and sweetest.

"Phoe-be," whistled Farmer Brown's boy once more and held out his hand. In it was a cracked hickory nut.

"Dee, dee, dee! See me! See me!" cried Tommy Tit and flitted down from the maple tree right on to the hand of Farmer Brown's boy, and his bright little eyes twinkled merrily as he helped himself to a bit of nut meat.

Peter Rabbit looked at Happy Jack, and Happy Jack looked at Chatterer, and all three acted as if they couldn't believe their own eyes. Then they looked back at Farmer Brown's boy, and there on his head sat Tommy Tit.

"Dee, dee, dee, chickadee! See me! See me!" called Tommy Tit, and his voice was merrier than ever, for he had made good his boast.

XXIII

Chatterer Grows Very, Very Bold

I'M NOT afraid. I am afraid. I'm not afraid. I am afraid. I'm not afraid."

Chatterer kept saying these two things over and over and over again to himself. You see, he really was afraid, and he was trying to make himself believe that he wasn't afraid. He thought that perhaps if he said ever and ever so many times that he wasn't afraid, he might actually make himself believe it. The trouble was that every time he said it, a little voice, a little, truthful voice down inside, seemed to speak right up and tell him that he was afraid.

Poor Chatterer! It hurt his pride to have to own to himself that he wasn't as brave as little Tommy Tit the Chickadee. His common sense told him that there was no reason in the world why he shouldn't be. Tommy Tit went every day and took food from the hand of Farmer Brown's boy. It seemed to Chatterer, and to Happy Jack the Gray Squir-

rel, and to Peter Rabbit, and to
Sammy Jay, and to Blacky the
Crow, all of whom had seen him
do it, as if it were the very brav-
est thing they ever had seen,
and their respect for Tommy Tit
grew wonderfully.

But Tommy Tit himself didn't
think it brave at all. No, Sir,
Tommy knew better. You see, he
has a great deal of common sense
under the little black cap he
wears.

"It may have been brave of me
to do it the first time," thought
he to himself, when the others
told him how brave they thought
him, "but it isn't brave of me

now, because I know that no harm is going to come to me from Farmer Brown's boy. There isn't any bravery about it, and it might be just the same way with Chatterer and all the other little forest and meadow people, if only they would think so, and give Farmer Brown's boy half a chance."

Chatterer was beginning to have some such thoughts himself, as he tried to make himself think that he wasn't afraid. He heard the door of Farmer Brown's house slam and peeped out from the old stone wall. There was Farmer Brown's boy with a big, fat hickory nut held out in the most tempting way, and Farmer Brown's boy was whistling the same gentle little whistle he had used when Chatterer was his prisoner, and he had brought good things for Chatterer to eat. Of course, Chatterer knew perfectly well that that whistle was a call for him, and that that big fat hickory nut was intended for him. Almost before he thought, he had left the old stone wall and was halfway over to Farmer Brown's boy. Then he stopped short. It seemed as if that little voice inside had fairly shouted in his ears: "I am afraid."

It was true; he was afraid. He was right on the very point of

That little voice inside had fairly shouted:
"I am afraid."

turning to scurry back to the old stone wall, when he heard another voice. This time it wasn't a voice inside. No, indeed! It was a voice from the top of one of the apple trees in the Old Orchard, and this is what it said:

"Coward! Coward! Coward!"

It was Sammy Jay speaking.

Now it is one thing to tell yourself that you are afraid, and it is quite another thing to be told by someone else that you are afraid.

"No such thing! No such thing! I'm not afraid!" scolded Chatterer, and then to prove it, he suddenly raced forward, snatched the fat hickory nut from the hand of Farmer Brown's boy, and was back in the old stone wall. It was hard to tell which was the most surprised—Chatterer himself, Farmer Brown's boy, or Sammy Jay.

"I did it! I did it! I did it!" boasted Chatterer.

"You don't dare do it again, though!" said Sammy Jay in the most provoking and unpleasant way.

"I do too!" snapped Chatterer, and he did it. And with the taking of that second fat nut from the hand of Farmer Brown's boy, the very last bit of fear of him left Chatterer, and he knew that Tommy Tit the Chickadee had been right all the time when he insisted that there was nothing to fear from Farmer Brown's boy.

"Why," thought Chatterer, "if I would have let him, he would have been my friend long ago!" And so he would have.

And this is all about Chatterer the Red Squirrel for now. Sammy Jay insists that it is his turn now, and so the next book will be about his adventures.